Enid Blyton's
Noddy
and the Magic Boots

D1096932

One afternoon when Noddy was out
walking by himself because it was such
a lovely day, he went into Be-Careful
Wood. Its name was a very good one . . .

Because you just had to be careful in that wood. All kinds of queer people lived there. There was Pop-Out who lived in a big oak tree with a door. Do you see it?

When Noddy went by, Pop-Out behaved like his name. He popped out of his tree with a yell and gave Noddy such a fright that he fell over – bump!

Another queer person who lived in Be-Careful Wood was Mr. Stumps. He could make himself look just like the stump of an old tree . . .

And when Noddy sat down on the strange little stump Mr. Stumps began to crawl away with Noddy. Oh dear, what a shock Noddy got! He got up and ran away quickly.

"Hallo – who's this coming along, smiling all over his face?" An old pedlar came along, carrying a big tray of goods in front of him. "Hullo," he said to Noddy. "I'm Mr. Grin. Can I sell you anything today? What about this hat?"

"No, thank you," said Noddy. "I like
my own hat. It's got a bell." "Well,"
said Mr. Grin, "what about a nice pair
of shoes? Yours are really very babyish,
you know."

"Dear me, are they?" said Noddy. "Well, perhaps I will try on a pair of shoes. These bright-green ones look nice." So he sat down to try them on – yes, they fitted well! "Stand up and walk about in the shoes," said Mr. Grin, smiling in a most friendly fashion.

"They're very cheap. They certainly suit you. Are they comfortable?" Noddy was walking about proudly. "Yes – they're lovely," he said. "Walk to that tree and back," said Mr. Grin. So Noddy set off to the tree – but what's this . . .

He couldn't walk back! He had to go walking on – and on and on. He couldn't stop! "Hey, there's a magic spell in these shoes!" shouted Noddy. "Tell them to walk back!"

Mr. Grin laughed and laughed. "Those shoes will take you to my master, Mr. Frown-Hard," he called. "I often get servants for him by this little trick. Goodbye!"

Well! Noddy could hardly believe his ears! To think that Mr. Grin had got him to try on a pair of shoes that had a walk-away spell in them – and now he was off to Mr. Frown-Hard!

Poor Noddy! Look at him walking on
and on, down this winding path and
that, through the trees, all by himself.
He can't stop. The shoes won't let him!

Noddy walked on till night-time
came and the moon came out. At last he
walked right out of Be-Careful Wood
and came to a small hill. On the top was
a cottage.

It had eight chimneys, and four doors in a row in the front. How queer! Was this where Mr. Frown-Hard lived? Yes – there he is, peeping out of the window, waiting for a new servant.

All the four doors flew open at once,
and the shoes took Noddy to one of
them. In he went. The doors shut. Oh
dear! Now how will anyone ever know
where little Noddy is?

Noddy's little car was lonely in its garage without Noddy. Where was he? Why didn't he come and drive it? Ah, here was somebody opening the garage doors . . .

But it wasn't Noddy. It was Big-Ears. Big-Ears had come to see why Noddy hadn't visited him. He was astonished to find that Noddy's house was empty.

And here he was, peeping in the
garage to see if Noddy had gone away in
his car. How surprised he was to see the
car there, all by itself, looking very sad.

"Something has happened to Noddy!" said Big-Ears. "Come along, little car. We'll go and look for him." So he got into the car and drove off. Parp-parp!

"Noddy always wanted to go to Be-Careful Wood, so maybe he went there," thought Big-Ears – and here he is, driving carefully through the wood.

Very soon they met a pedlar. It was Mr. Grin, with his tray of goods in front of him. "Buy, buy, buy!" he cried. And then Big-Ears saw something on the tray that made him stare!

What did Big-Ears see on Mr. Grin's tray? He saw Noddy's shoes, red with blue laces. In a trice he was out of the car and had got hold of Mr. Grin.

He shook him hard. "Where did you get those shoes? Tell me before I turn you into a stone and throw you in the stream! Quick, tell me!"

Mr. Grin forgot to smile. He went down on his knees and begged for mercy. "Don't put a spell on me. I'll tell you where I got them from. I will, I will!"

Soon Big-Ears knew how Noddy had put on the magic shoes and had to go on walking till he came to Mr. Frown-Hard's house. How he glared at Mr. Grin.

"Have you another pair of shoes with the same kind of spell in them? You have? Well, put them on – and lead us to Mr. Frown-Hard's cottage. Quick!"

And now here is poor Mr. Grin wearing magic shoes, plodding through the wood on his way to Mr. Frown-Hard's house. And after him goes Big-Ears in the car.

Now Big-Ears and Mr. Grin had come to Mr. Frown-Hard's cottage with its eight chimneys and four doors. Big-Ears knocks at every one of them in turn – blam-blam-blam-blam!

They all fly open at once! Big-Ears
goes in at one, Mr. Grin goes in at
another, and the little car drives itself in
at a third – parp-parp-parp!

Out of the fourth door rushes Mr. Frown-Hard in alarm. Look who is chasing him with a big broom – Little Noddy! Oh, how pleased he is to see dear old Big-Ears!

"We'll lock Mr. Grin in the house," said Big-Ears with a smile as broad as Mr. Grin's was. Slam, slam, slam, slam – all four doors were shut and locked.

And away drove Big-Ears and Noddy, with Mr. Grin peeping dolefully through a window. "He should be called Mr. Sulk now," said Noddy. "Oh, it is nice to be in my car again!"

Well, you can guess what a tea-party they had that day when they all got back to Big-Ears' house. Even the little car was allowed indoors. Parp-parp! What a treat!